Disney
Olaf's
FROZEN
ADVENTURE

By Amy Sky Koster

Illustrated by
the Disney Storybook Art Team

A GOLDEN BOOK • NEW YORK

Olaf burst out of a **KRANSEKAKE**. Pieces of cake fell every which way.

"Surprise!" he shouted.

"Olaf, not yet!" said Anna.

Elsa smiled. "The surprise holiday party starts *after* the Yule Bell rings."

It was Arendelle's first holiday season in forever, and the two sisters would be spending it with the people of their kingdom.

The castle courtyard was filled with festive townspeople. Excitement grew as Kristoff and Sven brought in the Yule Bell.

"The Yule Bell signals the start of the holidays in Arendelle," Elsa told Olaf.

"Okay . . . now," Anna whispered.

The bell rang out, and all the villagers cheered.

Bong!

Bong!

Bong!

"*Surprise!*" Olaf shouted to the crowd.

And with that, Elsa and Anna flung open the castle doors to invite everyone in. But instead of staying for the surprise party, the townspeople began to leave!

"Wait!" Anna said. "Going so soon?"

"The Yule Bell rang," replied one woman, "so I must get home for my family's tradition: rolling the **LEFSE**!"

"Our tradition is putting out porridge for the **TOMTE**," added a man.

"We're baking traditional **BORDSTABELBAKKELS**!" two sisters exclaimed.

Elsa invited a couple named Mr. and Mrs. Olsen to the castle, but they shook their heads.

"Thank you," said Mr. Olsen, "but Olga and I need to get home to knit socks for our grandchildren." He smiled. "And we wouldn't want to intrude on *your* family traditions."

With the villagers gone, the sisters needed some cheering up. Kristoff serenaded them with "The Ballad of Flemingrad," a traditional holiday song he had learned from the trolls. But it took a strange turn when he started singing about nostrils.

Then Kristoff revealed another odd troll tradition: Flemmy the Fungus Troll!

"Now you lick his forehead and make a wish!" Kristoff said.

"Whoa, gross," said Anna.

Everyone laughed.

Olaf followed the sisters into the ballroom. He couldn't wait to hear about their holiday tradition.

"Do we have any traditions from when we were little, Elsa?" asked Anna.

"After the gates were closed, we were never together," Elsa replied. "I'm sorry, Anna. It's my fault that we don't have a tradition."

Olaf realized that everyone in Arendelle had a holiday tradition— except Anna and Elsa.

The little snowman ran to the stables.

"Sven! Anna and Elsa don't have a holiday tradition."
Then he had an idea. "Let's go find the best tradition Anna
and Elsa have ever seen and bring it back to the castle!"

Olaf hooked Sven to Kristoff's sleigh, and the two
immediately set out.

Olaf knocked on the door of the first house they came to.

"What is your holiday tradition?" he asked a boy and his mother.

"We make candy canes together." The boy handed one to Olaf.

Olaf pulled out his carrot nose and popped in the candy cane.

His eyes whirled. "Ohhh, sugar rush!"

The boy stared at Olaf. "You're supposed to eat it."

"Eat my new nose? Why would I do that?" asked Olaf.

"Because it's that time of year!" the boy said.

Olaf and Sven stopped at home after home to learn
about the villagers' holiday traditions. Then they loaded
the sleigh with things to take back to Anna and Elsa.

At their last stop, Olaf found the entire Oaken family celebrating in the sauna. Olaf thought this was a great tradition . . .

so he added a portable sauna to the pile on the sleigh.

But hot coals from the sauna caused problems.
The sleigh caught fire! When it went over a cliff,
Sven and Olaf landed on opposite sides of a ravine . . .

. . . and all the holiday items they'd collected for Anna and Elsa were gone—except a fruitcake!

Olaf was still hopeful. But Sven was worried. He could hear wolves howling in the dark forest.

Back at the castle, Elsa found Anna
in the attic.

"What are you doing up here?"
she asked.

"Looking for traditions," said Anna.
She had been pulling items out of a trunk
filled with her childhood belongings.

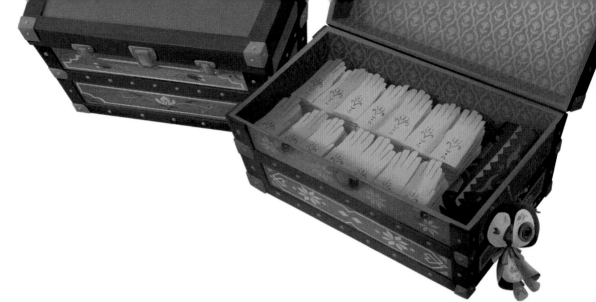

"What's in your trunk?" asked Anna.

"Mostly gloves," said Elsa. But as she reached into the trunk, she heard a ringing. She lifted out a small box with bells on top and handed it to Anna. When Anna opened it, she couldn't believe her eyes.

Suddenly, the two sisters heard a kerfuffle outside. They ran down to the stables, where Sven was trying to tell Kristoff something. The girls knew immediately what he was trying to communicate.

"Olaf is lost in the forest!" said Anna.

"And being chased by hungry wolves!" said Elsa.

The sisters had to gather everyone to search for Olaf right away.

Anna and Elsa headed into the forest, calling Olaf's name. Kristoff and Sven were close behind, with a search party of villagers.

"Olaf, where are you?" cried a worried Anna.

Just when they thought they'd never find him, the sisters spotted a carrot sticking out of a snowdrift. Olaf!

Olaf explained how he had collected traditional holiday items for the sisters but then lost them—even the fruitcake, which had been grabbed by a large bird.

"I'm sorry you still don't have a tradition," the little snowman said.

"But, Olaf, we do," said Anna. "Look!"

She opened the box with the bells on top and showed Olaf what was inside.

The box was filled with sketches Anna had made of Olaf when she was a little girl!

"You're the one who first brought Elsa and me together," said Anna.

"And kept us connected when we were apart," added Elsa.

"Every Christmas, I made Elsa a gift," Anna
continued. "It was always an image of you."
Elsa nodded. "And I saved every one of them."

"All those long years alone, we had you to remind us of our childhood," Elsa said.

"And how much we still loved each other," Anna agreed.

"It's you, Olaf! *You* are our holiday tradition,"
said Anna. *"Surprise!"*
The sisters hugged the little snowman.

Soon glowing lanterns emerged from the dark forest.
The villagers were relieved to see that Olaf was safe.
That was when Elsa had a brilliant idea.

Because it was Anna and Elsa's first winter holiday together in forever, the celebration had to be extra special. With a little help from the villagers, they hosted their big party after all, right there in the forest!

Anna and Elsa had rediscovered their holiday
tradition and started a new tradition for Arendelle.
They would plan a forest party every year—thanks to Olaf!

GLOSSARY

BORDSTABELBAKKELS (BOO-stah-bel-beck-els):
Norwegian table stacking cookies.

KRANSEKAKE (KRUN-suh-ka-kay):
A Danish and Norwegian wreath cake made
from rings of different sizes.

LEFSE (LEFS):
A traditional Scandinavian flatbread, usually made
around the holidays.

TOMTE (TOMT):
A mythological creature from Scandinavian folklore, typically
associated with the winter season.

ARENDELLE'S
TRADITIONAL HOLIDAY DECORATIONS

The ringing of the
Yule Bell—always at
noon—signals the start
of the winter holiday
season in Arendelle.

The animals on either side of the Yule Bell are called Yule goats.

The Arendelle wreath is hung as a decoration throughout the kingdom.

Look back through the pages of the story and see if you can spot images of the traditional bell, goat, and wreath.